AfroPoetic

Poems by
Jaylene Clark Owens

ISBN-13: 9781796302974

Cover design by Adam Woods
Edited by Laurence Owens and Tracey A. Casseus
Poet photo by Britney Marcel Photography

DEDICATION

*Laurencio, my husband, I couldn't do any of this without you.
Thank you for everything you are and everything you do.*

*My parents, Mommy and Daddy, without you, there is no me.
Thank you for always, always believing in my dream. You
provided the strong foundation that enabled me to grow.*

*My friends and family, my tribe, my core, y'all make a sista feel
so good with your continuous love and support.*

*Thank you GOD for blessing me with this gift. I pray you allow me
to continue sharing it with others.*

Table of Contents

Why Poetry 1

The D.O.C..4

The Train..7

SoHa..10

For Gabrielle..13

For a Dark Skin Girl.................................16

Oscar...20

Super Powers..22

Winter Advisory.....................................25

I Woke Up Like Dis..................................28

You Ugly..29

Land of the Free....................................31

Table of Contents

Sunshine..34

Haiku Love...35

Jeopardy...36

It's OK..38

Tree of Life...39

Passage..42

Body Positive..45

GenTro of the Dance Flo'.................................48

Popped Culture...50

Wakanda Forever..52

Over and Over Again......................................55

My Voice, My Choice......................................57

NOTE FROM THE POET

This is a collection of spoken word poems
Made for the stage
Now placed on the page
Enjoy it how you will, do ya own thing
But don't be afraid to read it out loud and hear the words sing!

♥♥♥♥♥♥♥

Why Poetry

When you ask me why I do poetry
This is exactly why
For the racist, prejudiced, pale, guys
Who would murder a young black girl by forcing her head
backwards into a pool of water
And then claim he was tryna baptize her
Rid her of all her innate sin
Rinse that dirt, filth, and trash off, which she calls skin
And make her pure
White as snow
Oh yeah! You didn't know?
Being Black is horrible
Black is the color of dirt
It's the color you wear to funerals when you're sad and hurt
Black is something you find on the bottom of your shoe
Underneath your nasty nail
And the color of your eye when you're beaten by a man because
you're a female
Black
Is the word "lack" with a "B"
Because people with that color should lack the ability to even be
Which is why when you see a group of Black kids just being
themselves and having fun
You immediately think crime scene
And find any reason on earth to pick one of them to quarantine
Like my girl who hopped the turnstile
While we were singing loud and laughing all the while
But you two racist pigs see us enjoying ourselves as an
"intimidation" to your dear White people
So you grab her up
Ready to hang that Black girl from a church steeple
But instead
You pull her to the side
And attempt to belittle and humiliate her as you piercingly look
into those soft, hazel eyes
Forget all your lies!
About how this is just your routine procedure
Are those the niggers comin'?
No, forget the summons
Put her hands behind her back

And forcefully slap those cold handcuffs around her small, gentle
wrists
"You have the right to remain silent through all of this"
Remain silent? Do you know who you're dealing with?
The only thing I have to write are these words in my head
"What? Are you going to do a little rap? I thought hip-hop was
dead?"

Humph, I spit flames you moron
But in an oxy-moron, I do it well
I spray the fire that extinguishes the heat of living in a
stereotypical poetic hell
I spit the fire that freezes the mind
Paralyzing your thoughts with my every line
Until you feel the chills run down your spine
And your thoughts become mine
I spit my poetry
I spit flames that will imprison you and put you in a
metaphorical, lyrical jail cell
And when you try to break free
The bars that I spit confine you and won't let you out cuz my
words hold the key
Keep throwing your racist thoughts at me
And I'll make sure my flames engulf you and burn you alive
Or I could just sit you in the audience and spit fireballs at you
while I'm rhyming on stage and I'm doing it live
Cuz I spit my poetry
I spit...
Nah, forget that
Let's go all out
I vomit my words into paper bag ears that are often deafened by
the constant rustling of nothingness
My mouth is a dragon ready to spit flames that would singe the
gates of hell
So run tell that to the judge
Cuz from my words, I will not budge
Is this all too much for you?
Am I spitting the truth too fast?
Are my words stinging your eyes like a literary sandblast?
It's OK, I'll wait for your brain to catch up to my intellectual flow

... wordsIwillnotbudge
Isthisalltoomuchforyou?
AmIspittingthetruthtoofast?
Aremywordsstingingyoureyeslikealiterarysandblast?

Good
Now that your brain is in sync with what I'm thinking
Let me reprogram some things
Black is beautiful
The color of the midnight sky on a starry summer night
The color of the berry when it's sweet, plump, and just right
Black are the words in all literature that enlightens women and men
And Black are my thoughts when I express them to my paper and pen
So no I'm not some rapper doing some silly little rap
And no I'm not a criminal just because I'm Black
I'm a poet
Spitting flames through my blowtorch pen until my fingers get blistery
Giving me the authority to say words in my piece like "simple-ly"
I write to express and relieve myself
That's why I do poetry

The D.O.C.

I am a member of the Diaspora of Color, aka the D.O.C.
This is one of my favorite parts of my ID
When God created the members that look like me, I imagine He
had a big pot
And He filled it with cocoa beans before the world knew what
cocoa beans were
And after the beans were ground I see Him holding the pot over
the sun
Which is why even today it takes a lot to make us burn
Often times we just glow
And I picture Him adding just a few red grapes and a sprinkle of
blueberries for our rich red, and sometimes blue, undertones
And I just see Him pouring it onto our bones
Like how you pour chocolate into a mold
And when our skin had set
I imagine Him saying,
"Wow. What a sight to behold."
And after He used His Earth to create all the different hues of the
world I imagine Him resting
Being grateful for His artistry
His mastery of color that made up the Diaspora
And I am so proud to be a part of it
Started in Africa now we here
And there
We, this colorful people, we are everywhere
We are gumbo in New Orleans
Pelau in Trinidad
Pollo guisado in DR
We are this stew
With thousands of flavors, and scents, and ingredients, but we are
all cooking over the same fire
And that fire is our history
Our history, burning, raging, so hot sometimes it's painful to look
at
Like how they tell you don't look directly into the sun because it
will burn your eyes
They say don't look directly into the African Diaspora history
because it might burn your mind
Might make you feel guilty if you're not a part of it, if your
ancestors were the cause of it

And if you're a member it might make you ashamed
Looking into that fire and seeing Black skin cackling, dangling from a tree
But that part of our history doesn't define we
We are more than slavery, and genocide, Jim Crow, and apartheid
We are art personified
Our music, our dance, our rhythms, our beats
Have influenced others all over this globe
We were the 1st so we set the standard, truth be told
But truth don't be told
Truth be buried down, down deep in the bowels of Africa
That's where truth be
Buried
But it's time for it to be resurrected
Cuz truth be told we are scientists, engineers, medical professionals, we are inventors
Innovating and creating since the dawn of time
We are the truth and the light
No, literally, the light
You couldn't see in this room if it wasn't for we
We all know about Thomas
Good ol' Con Edison
Pero con Edison was Lewis Howard Latimer, the African–American draftsman who worked with him
Edison is widely credited for the lightbulb but if it weren't for Latimer, by now this room would be dim
For Edison used paper filaments in his bulbs, which would burn out real quick
Whereas Latimer improved on the bulb by creating a carbon filament
And this enabled the bulb to stay on for a significantly longer time
And even though many people don't know who you are Latimer, your Diaspora is gonna make sure you continue to shine longer
Longer than just 28 days in February
Please
If you really want to highlight all the things the Diaspora has done for this world?
Forget month
We need Black History Century
And in addition to being innovative, intellectual, resilient people
...damn we sexy!

We are beautiful, we are gorgeous
Our women come in all shapes and sizes, but many of us are voluptuous
Our curves are like winding roads on our bodies and people of all colors love to drive their eyes up and down our highways
They get lip injections
Those are our luscious lips
They get butt enhancements
Those are our hips and dips
They Robin Thicke, Macklemore, and JT across our TV
Those are our rhythms and beats
They attempt to move their hips and "twerk"
Psh...we've been shaking our behinds since we could stand on two feet
It's fun to act like you're part of the D.O.C. as long as you're not actually in it
As long as you don't actually have to deal with the racial injustice that comes from having this Black skin
You want to be just dark enough so that others can tell you were vacationing in the Caribbean
So to stay safe non-D.O.C. members try us on for size
They get "ratchet" and wear "tribal" print skirts because those are so in
They appropriate our culture because at the end of the day they'll always have the benefit of having the appropriate skin
They walk a mile in our shoes until they stop making money or the road gets too treacherous
Not interested in our journey, they just know that their kicks look fabulous
But I am so proud that I don't have to pretend
I am a tried and true member of the D.O.C. and I will be one to the end
Cuz we are a people filled with joy, filled with pain, filled with splendor, filled with wonder
We are the past, we are present, we are the future, the D.O.C., Diaspora of Color

The Train

You are on the train
Surrounded by all the things that come with living in a metropolis
In this crowded subway car
Bookbags bang backs, kids colloquially curse cuz kids can, and
dudes display deplorable decorum
But you are used to all of that
You are used to the little White old lady clutching her purse a
little tighter when you enter the train
Used to the so, so, subtle surprise on the brow of the White man
next to you as you pull out your book on economic psychology
You are used to these things
Because they have always been
Since you've been riding the train with your mom as a little kid in
your skin
These things have always been
But something changed in 2001
A not so subtle change in what it means to be an American
In whom we are to fear
The word *terrorism* crashed into our ears and caused our trust in
Middle Eastern people to crumble
Our respect for our fellow Muslim Americans was hijacked and
replaced with hate
And the train bombings in Madrid in 2004 didn't make it no
better
And the train and bus bombings in London in 2005 didn't make it
no better
And Paris, and Kenya and Beirut and San Bernardino didn't make
it no better
So you are on the train
The doors open, the passengers squeeze in despite there being no
room
And a young Middle Eastern man stands next to you
His olive brown skin not too far from your chocolate brown skin
Just a few countries and histories away
Years ago, riding the train with your mom, you wouldn't have
thought twice about the "A-rab" standing next to you
But today is different
Today you look at him and get a lump in your throat
And you're so mad at yourself that that lump is there

7

Because you know that lump is no more than illogical fears balled up and held together by the media
So you attempt to swallow it
But on the way down it tightens your chest
And stiffens your back
And now your brain is thinking thoughts that you did not authorize

What if he has a bomb under his shirt?
Should I move? I don't want to get hurt
I can't move. That would be obvious
Isn't he too young to be a terrorist?
Maybe he recently got radicalized
Shit. I didn't even notice the bookbag there at his side
Why else would a Middle Eastern man have a bookbag on a train if not for a bomb?
Ok, just stay calm
Does he look like he could be a part of ISIS or the Taliban?
Oh my God! Am I starting to agree with 45's Travel Ban?
Ok, your fear is not real
Oh, God! He's reaching into his bag! Jesus, take the wheel!

And just like that, the train stops
And your Middle Eastern brother has just exited to go about his non-terrorist life
Your anxiety fades like the haircut of the brotha to your right
Relief quietly washes over you like water from a mother's cupped hand on a newborn's back
Your thoughts are filled with peace in the Middle Eastern man getting off the train
And as the crowd empties out of the subway car, you suddenly feel crowded
Available seats call you to rest, but you cannot get through
You cannot push past what is surrounding you
Shame
Shame engulfs you like a cold robe on a frigid night
Your cheeks feel hot
If not for your melanin your face would be beet red
As you think about how your brothas have been beat red, black, and blue by people holding racist stereotypes and fears that are now inside of...you
As the train doors close you catch your reflection

gasp You are the little White old lady clutching your chest just a little bit tighter when the Middle Eastern person enters the train
You are the White man with the so, so subtle surprise on your brow when the Middle Eastern man pulls out his book on succeeding in a Christian marriage
And for a second, you get it
For you it's only been a little over 17 years of illogical fears, but for them it's been a lifetime
For a second you understand how someone can just spill out stereotypes
When for a lifetime the world has poured them out so many negative stories, lies, and images that they don't have room enough to receive
But then you remember that you have a voice
And allowing this imperfect world to make you ignorant is a choice
So you are on the train
And a Middle Eastern man enters and sits next to you
Your sub-conscious is spilling out images of 9/11 and last night's news
But what is your conscious going to do?
Next stop: The Promised Land

SoHa (From *Renaissance in the Belly of a Killer Whale*)

I am from Harlem
I say it every chance I get
I love the sound of that name playing beats on my ear drums
I love the way it rolls off my lips
Haaaaarlem
When you say it you gotta make sure your breath don't stink
But it never does
It smells like barbeques in the park that last to the brink of dawn
It smells like that boy named Sean who you split your first
nutcracker with
Harlem
That Dutch name
Is where I played every double dutch game
Sang every 90's song
Where I knew if I ordered cheese eggs and grits from Pan-Pans, I
couldn't go wrong
That's *my* 'hood
Harlem
Yes, that's what it's called
That is its name
You shouldn't call it out of it
That's why it's called the *Harlem* Renaissance
Because so many talented and intellectual Black folks came out of
it
Which is why I—I just don't understand
How some people are trying to turn my home's name into a brand
Trying to box it
And squeeze it into some four letter package
Being from "SoHa" was not, and never will be, part of my
heritage
SoHa?? Really?!
So let me get this straight
You can spell it out to small businesses that they need to pack
their stuff to make way for your high rises that just can't wait
But when it comes to spelling out the name of this place you're
trying to profit off of you decide to abbreviate?
Oooooh gentrification
I'll call you GenTro
You pulled this mess in the Cast Iron District and called it SoHo
But Harlem is no ho

She will not sell her name for money
So calling her SoHa is a no go
You want to dabble in neo-soulfood
Living the champagne life while eating things you can't get at
Whole Foods
But if you're going to come here then call it for what it is
Harlem needs to tell you like an ol' skool mother would tell her
kids
"As long as you live under my roof, you'll abide by my rules
If ya think you gon' call me out my name in my own house??
A-huh-huh! Then y'all some fools"
That's what I think she should say
Because there will never be a time nor day
When I believe that calling Harlem, SoHa, is okay
Calling it SoHa
Is a big faux pas
You must be crazy, lady
Spitting all that gaga
Baby
It's Spanish Harlem, not SpaHa
Where young girls where chancletas and abuelas shout "Wepa!"
By calling it SoHa or SpaHa you aim to make people forget that
they once thought if they came to Harlem they would hear blah-
kah
Get shot like "Haha
I shot you cuz I'm Black and that's what we do"
By calling it SoHa or SpaHa you aim to make it sound chic, hip,
and cool
Like in every Harlem apartment there's a security camera and a
doorman in the vestibule
But if you ask me, nothing sounds cooler than living in Harlem
The home of the New Negro Arts Movement
If I wasn't from here, yet wanted to move here, it would be the
culture and history that would make me choose it
Not the actual ridiculous names that I've heard like SoHa, and
SoMar and E-Ha and We-Ha
No Ha's
Just Harlem
This is not about saying this one is not welcome or that one is
taking control of our neighborhood
It's not about pointing fingers or assigning blame
We welcome positive change in Harlem

But if you're going to come here, live here, see here, at least have the decency to call her by her name
Harlem

For Gabrielle

As my friend Candace said
"Y'all don't deserve Gabby Douglas"
Y'all don't deserve how she back bended into your living rooms
Triple twist flipped your TV screens to reveal mirrors in which
you could see your sorry selves reflected
So your daughters could see themselves reflected on an
international scene
She has had to overcome mountains of obstacles to get where she
is today
A 3x Olympic gold medalist who knows how to stick her dismount
But dis mountain is one she should have never had to climb and
it's got her stuck
Stuck in her feelings like a fruit fly in honey
Trying to fly high off the sweetness of her victory
But her surroundings keep pulling her down
You haters keep pulling her down
Y'all don't deserve Gabby Douglas
This young Queen is seated on a throne at the edge of history
Looking below at the past she becomes Narcissus without the pool
She cannot see herself reflected
Searching for a female All-Around Champ of color from any
nationality would yield no results
So she had to be the first
Edging out competition from the greatest gymnasts in the world
Yet y'all talkin' 'bout her edges
Numerous Black women online publicly criticizing her hair
Comin' for her crown
But I guess that's easy when you were never made to feel like
royalty
We have to do better
Lack of Black on Black shine is the true Black on Black crime
For when we strengthen our own radiance, the world has no
choice but to see our brilliance
No choice but to believe in our Black Girl Magic
So they train us to find ugliness in ourselves to make our beauty
disappear
Why y'all tryna make this young woman's greatness disappear?
Y'all don't deserve Gabby Douglas
She is a USA Olympian
Flying Squirrel mastering the uneven bars

But the way this country's White privilege is set up, the Olympics produce uneven stars
Endorsements on endorsements but Gabby could not afford to laugh during the anthem
Her skin color doesn't come with that kind of currency
Instead of placing her hand over her heart, she stood at attention
To honor a country that pays women who look like her little attention
Her name was dragged through the mud on social media like the body of James Byrd Jr.
Instead of hiding behind sheets, now they hide behind tweets
How dare you question Gabby's patriotism? She literally has USA GOLD in her last name
Y'all don't deserve Gabby Douglas
As if all that wasn't enough, y'all hit her with the oldest Black girl critique in the book
"She just didn't seem happy enough"
She didn't smile enough
She didn't stand enough
She didn't cheer enough
Just being a Black girl is rarely enough
If ya not smiling, ya angry
If you're too real, you're aggressive
If you're too dark, you gotta be light
Enough!
Gabby, you are enough
Not making it into the Rio All-Arounds must have been like winning a Tony for a role you were born to play
And then when the show is remounted, not making it past the first round of auditions
I can't imagine what my face would have looked like
But I saw you
Maturity crept into the corners of your mouth and lifted up your smile
The camaraderie in your left palm continuously pressed against the sportsmanship in your right as you applauded the teammates who advanced instead of you
And boo
You did it, not only as a true athlete, but as a Black woman filled with grace
And you are amazing
You owed them NOTHING

But you apologized just for being who you are
And baby girl, you are a star
You are loved
Them haters don't deserve you, but no matter what they say,
history will preserve you
You are a Queen
Forget them haters
They just mad cuz your crown is so golden
Just like them three medals you holdin'
We love you, Gabrielle ♥

For a Dark Skin Girl

He said, "You pretty for a dark skin girl"
Not just pretty walking through the city
"You pretty for a dark skin girl"
"Yo, check out Chocolate...she bad for a dark skin chick"
Only the chocolates deserve such a bittersweet, backhanded,
compliment
Where is your pride? Where is your dignity?
How dare you fix your lips to say a "compliment" that
simultaneously insults and degrades your entire identity?
"For a dark skin girl" like we are second rate
Like our skin they don't appropriate
Like it don't help shield us from the sun like a breastplate
Like its glow don't captivate
Must I continue to elaborate?
"For a dark skin girl" is a qualifying statement
Qualifying my beauty through your colorist preference for lighter
pigment
But clearly you are not qualified to talk to me about *any* standards
of beauty
When you boldly place me into this substandard aesthetic
category
That includes the women in your family who you clearly do not
show glory
For if you glorified them you would find beauty in their image
Full lips with gorgeous ebony skin would be a familiar visage
But instead, you basically say, "You pretty for someone who looks
something like my sister"
But your sister looks just like you so what are you really saying
about yourself, mister?
After years of hearing similar words over and over again my heart
has formed a blister
Like the ones you find on the bottom of a dancer's feet
After years of injuries, the hard, calloused skin makes the pain
obsolete
But every now and again you'll get a pain in just the right place
That will make you remember what you went through to get that
blister in the first place
And it takes me back to 8th grade, Harlem, when I was in middle
school

Where you were cool as long as you weren't on the receiving end of the class clown's ridicule
And like many 8th grade girls, I had a crush on a boy, we'll call him John
And we flirted here and there and I thought we were forming a bond
Until one day John dropped a bomb
It exploded in my face and made my skin turn to soot
Because John and his two friends started teasing me about how my skin looked
It was really John's friend who was the ring leader, we'll call him Price
And for the school year I paid to be the chimp in their 3 ring circus, I was the object of their vice
They tagged me as "it" and I had nowhere to run for base
They called me Ethiopia because it means "burnt face"
Price created a little jingle and I remember the words even still
He said, "A yo, you Black, with Similac on your grill"
That doesn't even make sense!!
How did I allow that to happen??
I remember when he came up with it while he was "freestyle rappin'"
It was so simple and stupid, yet people found it hilarious
Amazing how a foolish, incomplete, wack rhyme could be so nefarious
But here's the kicker ready to make a field goal for Team Irony
John and Price were just as dark as me!
In fact, Price was slightly darker...I remember we did the fist test
The evidence was right there and he still didn't wanna confess
To this "crime" of having dark skin
Outwardly projecting his self-hatred on me so he didn't have to address it within
Maaaaannnn, White people really did a number on us
Between slavery, and the constant preference for European standards, they just got us all messed up
Slavery got us stuck in this house vs. field nigger mentality
When being closer to Massa in hue made you betta, yet still a nigga, but in actuality
There is nothing about dark skin that makes you less than
My Black is equal to your Black
In fact it is greater than
All these one sided beauty campaigns you see on TV

Greater than us frequently being cast as the maid, the slave, the ghetto girl, the Mammy

Greater than light women getting 12% less jail time than dark ones just for being a lighter shade

Greater than not being able to hide my pain because I can't find a dark colored Band-Aid

And I know what you'll say, slavery ended so long ago

Hollywood loves dark skin women...just look at Lupita Nyong'o

But if you're gonna use Lupita to signify progress then you just don't get it

White America gawks at Lupita because they feel she looks exotic

Always "stunning" or "breathtaking" or "my God she is so beauteous"

But never "hot" or "sexy" because they feel her beauty is rare when in fact it's ubiquitous

Millions of Black girls grow into Lupitas, but they are rarely seen

Because this world makes it so difficult for a dark skin girl to appear on your screen

And if there are any dark skin little girls under the sound of my voice, I want you to do something for me

Take my voice and wrap it around you like your favorite blankie

And take these words with you wherever you go

Your Black is beautiful despite the status quo

Your Black is valid, your Black is gorgeous

The world is selling you this lie that your skin is ugly and you cannot afford this

Be proud in your Brown

Don't you dare hang your head down

Your skin is made of that of queens

Your skin gave birth to all human beings

You got that Black girl magic and they wonder what's your secret to make your skin glow

They ask why Black don't crack, they wanna bottle that, but they'll never know

Princess, they say your skin looks like dirt, that your father must have did your mother dirty to get you as a daughter

Next time you say, "Nah, I'm a child of God and this skin is like rich soil filled with holy water

Melanin in my cells is what makes me brown like a coconut when it is ripe and mature"

And you tell them, "You are too green and naïve to understand the complex simplicity of the beauty I have in store"

And baby girl, the next time they do that doll test
And they ask you which doll is the prettiest
You pick the one that is most brownie, brown sugared, chocolatey
And when they ask you why, say, "Because that baby doll looks like me"
Tell them, "I believe I'm one of the prettiest girls in the world
Despite life makin' it hard out here for a dark skin girl"

Oscar

#OscarsSoWhite
And I'm as angry as a colorless Grouch
Because I want to see myself reflected as I watch from my couch
I want to see people who look like me excelling in my field
And not just for stereotypical roles where we are enslaved people excelling in the field
And this is not to diminish those who have played those roles, for they have done them masterfully
This is just me speaking my truth unabashedly
We can play so much more than subservient
Frequently cast in parts low on the totem pole, when we can master roles that are salient
#OscarsSoWhite
Like a whiteout, which is a weather condition
In which visibility and contrast are severely reduced by the white snow, that's the definition
Like how our visibility is limited to hosting, singing, dancing, or presenting
We can be funny, shuck and jive, but not be recognized for the work we do, which is acting
And it's hard for aspiring Black actors to see opportunity on the horizon when the whiteout is so strong
When they have no reference points and can't see any signs that they belong
#OscarsSoWhite
Like the inside of a bottle of Wite-Out
Someone call Shonda Rhimes to be the correctional fluid of the movie industry, send her on the next flight out
Cuz she gets it, diverse casts, Black women in complex leading roles, bringing the real world to TV
Although we get a lil shine and some White folks think it's too much, like in that ignorant Deadline article written by someone named Nellie
#OscarsSoWhite
Cuz the Oscars are just a symptom, but we need to attack the disease
Though vital to your career, it's just an awards show...can we see the big picture, please?
There are not enough Blacks in big pictures, and when we're in one, it's rare it gets its proper kudos

Number 1 at the box office for weeks, but all it does is make money for the studios
Black buying power is expected to reach 1.2 trillion this year, but I feel like we're invisible, man
Feeling like Ralph Ellison in "Invisible Man"
"I am invisible, understand, simply because people refuse to see me"
Like how Creed was written by, directed by, and based on Black men, yet all they saw was Rocky
The Oscars have had a rocky relationship with Black folks over time
With only 15 awards going to Black people since 1939
With most of those going to Black women who were the Best Supporting Actresses in their movies
Which is no surprise since the backs of female Blacks have been supporting this country for centuries
Only ONE Black woman has won for Best Actress and that was Ms. Halle Berry for Monster's Ball
I just wish I didn't have to see Halle bare it all
Begging for the White man to make her feel good
And we as actors of color will not beg the Academy to recognize us because it diminishes our integrity and selfhood
But we will demand respect, fairness, inclusion, and opportunity
Cuz they are from Motion Picture Arts and Sciences, but I am from Frederick Douglass Academy
In Harlem they taught me that without struggle there is no progress
And the Oscars may be a struggle now, but if we keep making our voices heard, they can't keep blocking our shine, for we are luminous
Black absorbs light and is the absence of color, so really #OscarsSoBlack
Huh. Look at that
And white reflects light and is the presence of all colors, interesting fact
So in the coming years if they say #OscarsSoWhite
It better be because there was a presence of all colors, black, white, brown, red, yellow, cuz only then will they get it right

Super Powers

Some White people possess super powers
Not all
But *some* White people possess superpowers
It's actually quite amazing to see
This super power comes from their ability to see
And hear
And it can be activated by a myriad of things such as guilt, rage, ignorance, or fear
It's kind of like pareidolia, the imagined perception of a familiar pattern or meaning where it does not actually exist
Like seeing the face of a man in the moon, the Virgin Mary in your grilled cheese, or Jesus in your fried fish
But with this White power, their imagined perception of a familiar pattern of racist stereotypes causes them to see things that are not there, to hear words that have not been said
Pareidolia can get you featured on the news, so can this White superpower, except you'll be dead
Officer Betty Shelby utilized this superpower when she saw Terence Crutcher reach for a gun that he did not possess
I imagine that on her cornea the image of the scary Black man from her nightmares, and the Black man in front of her began to coalesce
Her cornea led to his coroner
Man, it must be nice to have people with vision like that in your corner
Some officers saw an 18-year-old when briefly looking at 12-year-old Tamir Rice
What an incredible power to be able to see years he will never add to his life
But it's not just vision...the superpower extends to their ability to hear
I guess it's kind of like how certain whistles can only be heard by a dog's ear
So I guess Carolyn Donham was being a real bitch when she claimed to hear the whistle that made Emmett go still
The reason some White people hear "White Lives don't matter" when Black people say ours do, is that because we say it real shrill?
Are we saying it at such a high register that normal people just can't hear the sound?

Or could it be, and this is crazy, that we are actually just saying our lives matter and that in itself is profound?
Could it be that we are simply saying our lives matter too?
Dear White people, everything isn't always about you!
You hear "Black Girls Rock" and deem it racist because your superpower ears hear "...and White girls do not"
But this world doesn't make you question whether they do, that's like asking if fire is hot
That's like asking if Black women earn less than White women just for having melanin...of course they do!
Like asking if Black women have to work 7 months into the year just to make what a White man made in the previous one
Yes, that's true too!
Black women work the most hours, earn less, and are the most educated group in the USA
Yet your superpower vision can't see that
Oh yes, some White people can see things that are not there, but when it comes to seeing the facts, they're as blind as a bat
Black women with advanced education make $7 an hour less than White men with only a Bachelor's Degree
Even in our excellence we are valued as less than their mediocrity
Abigail Fisher couldn't see the 42 White students admitted to University of Texas who performed academically worse than she did
Didn't matter that her grades weren't great, she just couldn't see how they could deny her, yet admit a Black kid
Because what's the point of having skin that easily burns if you can't use it for white hot privilege?
It's privilege that allows you to watch that old Procter and Gamble commercial about bias and say none of it is true
Because fearing that your child may not come home because of the color of their skin is not something you had to do
When Colin Kaepernick says he's protesting the oppression and police brutality against Black and Brown people by taking a knee
Some White folk use their superpowers to hear that he is against troops fighting for this country
So now they burning their sneakers and cuttin' the checks off their Nike
When they should be cuttin a check to a therapist to unpack the racial bias embedded in their psyche
Cuz when you have super power from colonizing and enslaving Black people to build your empire

Your descendants get superpowers that allow them to see and hear whatever they desire

Like, despite my repetition of "some White people" there are those who will hear this and say I'm racist

Others will feel the need to say "not all White people..." even though I never said this

Don't waste your energy trying to convince me these superpowers don't exist, cuz that's bull

Instead, please figure out how to deactivate them in yourselves and your peers, because that would be super powerful

Winter Advisory

Thanks, Key and Peele
I'm Lisette and there's a winter advisory in effect for the next 24
hours across our entire region
Plummeting temperatures and freezing rain will cause our
normally safe neighborhoods, streets, and roads to become
extremely dangerous due to the presence of Black ice
Not to be confused with regular ice, or clear ice, Black ice is
extremely dangerous and life-threatening
Black ice, it's worth mentioning
Is known to rob innocent victims at dawn and late in the evenings
Robbing people of their balance and causing them to lose their
personal belongings
So hold on tight to your purses, ladies, if you see any ice that's
Black
This fluffy, white snow can look so beautiful, but this ugly black
ice is one of its drawbacks
The tricky thing about Black ice is that it's invisible
It can be all around us, yet imperceptible
Not able to be seen, that is, until it gets violent
There aren't many good things to say about Black ice so when it
comes to reporting on that we mostly remain silent
We usually cast Black (g)ice in a negative light, which is right
Since they--it is so dangerous and dark, it can't be seen in the
limelight
It can't be in prime time, getting shine
We only report on Black (g)ice being menacing and that's just fine
Here with me now I have one of the victims of Black (g)ice,
Rebecca Lori
Rebecca, please, tell us your story

So last week I was jogging in my neighborhood, which is usually
safe any time of the day
Safe like, moms are not even scared to send their kids out to play
So I was jogging and I didn't even see the Black (g)ice
I just screamed and tasted blood after I slipped like twice
Now I'm scared of all Black (g)ice, no matter the shape
I wish the police could capture all the Black (g)ice, like maybe put
up some caution tape?
So take it from me, I should know
Stay far away from the Black (g)ice, only go near the white snow

Thank you, Rebecca
Be careful out there because as you can see, the damage Black
(g)ice can do is quite vast
Now here's Brenda in Studio One with the rest of this week's
forecast
Brenda?

Yeah...this is Brenda reporting live
I just want to take a few moments and talk a little more about the
Black (g)ice
We make Black (g)ice synonymous with menacing, threatening,
and dangerous
It's not just ice, but the Black ice that will endanger us
We illicit fear in the hearts of America when it comes to Black ice
Unfortunately we do the same damn thing when it comes to Black
guys
The scariest thing about the two? Their invisibility
Millions of Black and brown men disappear into the prison
system until all you can see is their profitability
Most national surveys don't account for prison inmates, resulting
in gross misrepresentations of US political, economic, and social
conditions
Throw Black guys in jail and they becomes Caspers: friendly
apparitions
Because when incarcerated they are no longer scary...out of sight,
out of mind
In society they're like a tumor, malignant, but behind bars Blacks
be benign
Behind bars, many Black bodies find themselves in the same
predicament
Where institutionalized and systemic racism has led to their false
imprisonment
Rendering them invisible in the lives of their families
Mothers without sons and Black kids without their daddies
Like Black ice, it's dangerous when Black guys can't be seen
Many Black boys grow up seeing dope dealers as the money
makers and either athletes or rappers on the covers of magazines
But just imagine the outcome if Black boys were surrounded by an
abundance of Black men to look up to
Like more Black men in the classroom, because right now their
percentage is only two

If more Black boys saw more Black men as teachers, and doctors, and engineers, then they would want to be those things too
Which is why it was so incredible and life changing to see Obama in the White House, but there's still so much work to do
And we will not pretend
Like the onus doesn't also fall on our Black men
They no longer own us so you can be an upstanding citizen
Instead of up standing on the block, selling rocks, like the street corner's denizen
Black men are so much more than that
Education be a fence
This game of life will not be fair but education can be your defense
Make the block hot because of the number of degrees
BFA, MBA, PhDs
Black men need two more levels of education to have the same chances of landing a job as a White man
And if they have the same level of education, the Black man will typically earn less than the White man can
Let's put down this belief that picking up a book is acting White
No my brotha, that is acting right
So yes America, you should be scared of the Black guys
After this I'm gonna kick it back to you Lisette
Cuz a brotha with an education, that's the real threat

I Woke Up Like Dis

I woke up like dis
Hair twisted or braided or in bantu knots
Scarf wrapped around my head
I like to think it's protecting my hair and my thoughts
Breath hot like fire, husband thinks it's a crying shame
I just tell him it's my mouth pre-heating so I can get ready to spit
these flames
No makeup when I wake up
But he finds me most beautiful in the morning when my face is
not caked up
I'm radiant, unadulterated Black Girl Magic beaming
I see so much possibility in each day, that's why my eyes be
gleaming
I pick out my hair because it grows up and not down
Defying gravity and haters, I have a built-in crown
I woke up like dis
Crust, pimples, bad breath, and all
My so called flaws don't make me feel small
They make me, me
And with them, I feel 20 feet tall

You Ugly

America, you are ugly without your makeup on
Not so beautiful when you wipe off the blood that makes your lips ruby red
That Freedom shade you use for your eyeshadow has worn away
Your somber eyes shadow hatred, watching its every move
Its color is all over you
The American Dream is no more than a caked on foundation you use to cover your blemishes
And now, wow, all your blemishes are popping out
You have no coverage
Have you seen the latest coverage?
Your imperfections dominate world news
You are ugly without your makeup on
Your makeup came in many different forms
It was the civil rights movement, it was the right to vote, it was affirmative action, it was the Obamas
It was these things that made the disillusioned believe we were post-racial
Many of your own people believed you were post-racial because a Black man was your president
But he was just your concealer attempting to hide the racism buried deep, deep, down in your pores
And his Black head could do nothing to remove the dirt that you've done and continue to do
America, you are ugly without your makeup on
Many of us
The Black, brown, yellow, impoverished, plenty of us
Knew your façade was a farce
Knew Equality was a lipstick we couldn't always find in our shade
But sooo many believed
Oooo, so many believed we were beyond racism
So many wished we would just get over slavery and move on
Believed that Racism was this discontinued mascara you might find online, but its presence wasn't prevalent
And then came Donald Trump
The best makeup remover America has ever had
That orange bottle contains some powerful stuff!
The discontinued Racism was put back on the shelf
Islamophobia, homophobia, xenophobia, became sores festering on your skin

Blistering
Oozing out division throughout your states
Your skin riddled with misogynists
Black and blue with bruises from the uptick in hate-crime related violence
But I've never seen you look so clear
I can see your true colors shining through
And they are ugly, but they are you
I've never seen racism paraded so proudly in my lifetime
Embraced so boldly
It was like overnight we got the alt-right and White folks throwing up Nazi salutes
But I rather a monster than a wolf in sheep's clothing
Yes, America!
Use that Trump Makeup Remover to show us who you really are
For we can't address the problem if we don't believe it's there
You are exposed
And everyone is seeing how you look in the morning
I just pray us Americans will wake up out of our mourning
It ain't over
We just need to give this country a makeover

Land of the Free

And now, please raise a fist for the singing of the second half of
the third verse of the National Anthem of the United States of
America:

No refuge could save the hireling and slave
From the terror of flight or the gloom of the grave
And the star-spangled banner in triumph doth wave
O'er the land of the free and the home of the brave

Land of the free, huh
I'd like to go there someday
I'd like to walk those streets
Freedom greeting me on every corner like
How are YOU today?
You don't have to be scared today
We removed those target dots clogging the pores of your melanin
You are free to live today
And tomorrow
And the next
So go on sell your CDs, play your music loud, throw your hands in
the air
And wave 'em like you just don't care
You won't get a bullet in your chest today
Land of the free, huh
I'd like to enroll my daughter in school there someday
Where the principal's locs will be down to her butt
And one of the school's principles will be that all students can
wear their hair as they please
My daughter's crown will not be compromised
She'll have the freedom to be a queen
Yeah, I'd like to go there someday
Instead I live in the United States of America
Where even the name is a lie, for we are not united
I don't know that I've seen this country more divided
I'd love to live in a country where love trumps hate
Instead I live in a country where voters love Trump's hate
Where freedom of speech and protest is a constitutional right
Until they declare what you're protesting is not right
So they burn the jersey of Colin Kaepernick

Because he doesn't want to stand and honor a country where it's ok to cap-a-nig
Who's unarmed with his hands up
Don't shoot the White man though
The bull's eye on Black bodies sees the Whites need to be handled with care in the arresting cycle so
Set the stakes to low
Don't mix your coloreds with the whites
The privilege they're dipped in is delicate so don't wring out any bullets
Wrap them first in a vest
Even though Dylan Roof murdered 9 praying Black folks in church, he is still a White prince
Do you dare disrespect him? No way!
So you get him a Whopper from Burger King to remind him of his royalty and that he can always have it his way
Way, way back in 1814, the anthem was just a new poem written by Francis Scott Key
Who said Black folks are, "a distinct and inferior race of people, which all experience proves to be the greatest evil that afflicts a community"
Yeah, the man was deep
Deep in his feelings because of the fierce group of about 6,000 formerly enslaved Blacks called the Colonial Marines
Who turned their backs on America to fight against the US on the side of the British
Backs that were broken, cut open, by men who called them their property
So clearly
They had no incentive for staying
The Brits promised the Blacks liberty for their service so they were literally fighting for freedom
Those Black men went from rags and making them riches
To red coats and causing them stitches
If I sing of the home of the brave, those are the men I imagine them to be
But Francis Scott was singing in a different key
Singing of the pride in the murder of Black bodies
Of fathers, never to return to their families
Of not having refuge from the gloom of the grave
Was he singing of _____,* or was he singing of a slave
But he had a right to write his poem, the 1st stanza, the 3rd, all of it

Just as I have a right to write mine and sing no parts of his
So thank you, Colin Kaepernick, for evoking the spirit of Tommie
Smith and John Carlos on a multi-billion dollar stage
Where many douse you with vitriol for not behaving like a
compliant little monkey in your NFL owner's cage
They won't show us footage of a crazed fan running across the
field
But an hour later, the same channel will show a Black man
bleeding to death behind his steering wheel
I saw a Snapchat from a college student calling three Eagles
players niggers for raising their fists during the anthem
Said, "If you don't like this country then get the hell out." Said a
bullet in the head was needed for each of them
You know who else felt the same way? Francis Scott Key
Co-founder of the American Colonialization Society, he believed
the solution was sending free Blacks "back" to their country
Their continent, of Africa, their home
A land from which their ancestors came from but which they had
never known
I saw this thinking as a freshman on campus too
In a bathroom stall, I was appalled, "Niggers go back to Africa
and take your spics with you"
I may have deep-seated hatred for some of the ways of this
country, especially its racism
But because cotton was deep-seeded and picked it grew into what
we now call capitalism
This global super power that you are allowed to savor
Was a product of, built by, funded by enslaved labor
So I will not get the hell out because I don't like how we as
America's sponsors are being treated
I will continue to speak up and write poems because discussion is
needed
Action is needed, change is needed
So go on Kaepernick, and the growing list of others, continue to
take a knee
Let us unite these states through our demand for change, let us
have solidarity
Until then, miss me, with tryna get me, to sing the words of
Francis Scott Key
I'm too busy tryna unlock this door to get into the land of the free

insert the name of the latest Black victim of police brutality

Sunshine

Poet's suggestion: Play "Everybody Loves the Sunshine" by Roy Ayers when reading this poem*

Folks get down in the sunshine
But what I love most is how my folks get brown in the sunshine
You mighta heard it through the grapevine
But I'm here to confirm, the darker the berry the sweeter the juice
Sweet like honey...chile get into this melanin that the sun helps me produce
I wish you could feel what I feel in the sunshine
The heat of my Virgin Island ancestors burning through my bloodline
In the sunshine, the spotlight, is where my people belong
They say darkness can't be bright, but look how they so wrong
Cuz we out here radiating
They say our skin is ugly, then jump in a tanning booth imitating
We jump in a booth creating
Poems and songs to lift us up when folks is out there hating
Aahh! The sunshine!
You got yours and I got mine
Sometimes it is the literal sun
Permeating me with Vitamin D, maintaining my circadian rhythm
Other times my husband is my sunshine
He is hot, makes me sweat cuz he's so fine
His chocolate melts my heart whenever I am with him
He is the shining star at the center of my solar system
But it's not just physical
Mentally, he stimulates me
He is my sun providing me with energy
To believe in what I see
When my reflection looks back at me
Black Girl Magic
Now, he sees me, when others don't, that's true
My sunshine boo
Who or what brings sunshine to you?
No matter what it is, don't let nobody take it away
Cuz we don't just shine some of the time, we were born this way
From our ancestors to our future girl and boy heirs
Continue to shine bright and live life in the sunshine like Roy Ayers

Haiku Love

5 relationships
7 years sinking...but you?
5 years of pure bliss

Black man you are king
Afro crown, your blood royal
Your skin majestic

I think about you
575
Times a day...that's love

My heart thumps in the
Syllabic beat of your name
You make me pulsate

We don't know the time
No need...we have forever
5:75

Your kiss waters me
It hydrates my pink flower
I bloom just for you

I would still love you
If all we had left was just
$5.75

Jeopardy

What is it about our skin that causes you to turn it into fly paper?
In White spaces, Black skin turns sticky
It traps all of your assumptions that buzz around us like flies
Until we are covered in so many of your irrational fears that we
morph into your worst nightmare
And your worst nightmare (Donald) trumps King's best dream
He dreamed that the sons of former slaves and former slave
owners will be able to sit down together at the table of
brotherhood
But we can't even sit down to a table at Starbucks without being
judged by the color of our mocha colored skin
Being dark and strong, size tall might get us a double shot
between the ribs because you wanna call the cops expresso
You don't wait
You serve coffee straight black, no cream to White men
But when we come in serving straight Black, no crime you begin
to question our motives
Like why are *you* here?
In our space
It's like us Black people must show a sticker of approval from a
White person to justify our existing in a predominately White
place
Like, you cannot park your Black body here for free if your
parking is not validated
If you don't validate your existence you must pay a fee
You must pay the price
Of humiliation, time wasted, frustration
Because you decided to take a nap in the common room
Black girl, you ain't nothing but common
Huh
But I'll ask you like Deena asked Effie
Now who you callin' common, you self-indulgent, self-absorbed,
unprofessional?
Did you feel empowered when you used your precious, privileged,
pointer finger to dial 911?
If the police don't catch you, Becky will, so run, nigger, run
But for your information, 311
Jim Crow is done
So wherever you see my face becomes a Black space

Like this place, here, where the gravity of the truth in my words
pulls you in so much that not even your White can get out
That's a black hole
You call the cops, might see a hole in one
Because you t'd off
At these Black women tryna tee off at your exclusive White golf
course
Of course, adjusting to things you are not used to can be difficult
But baby, you gon' get this change cuz no one likes a tattletale
toddler sittin' in its own BS
Much love to my brothas and sistas out West
Who used Becky's nonsense as fuel for the fire
That stoked the coals
That cooked up the Blackest Oakland BBQ story ever told
That's why it was lit
White people, stop calling the cops on Black folks just trying to
exist
You feel uncomfortable or like your life is in jeopardy
So you unjustifiably call the police on Black people thus putting
their lives in actual jeopardy
Alex, I'll take racial stereotypes for 200
"This type of person is Black, wearing casual clothing, and
minding their damn business in a predominately White space"
What is "a thug?" EHHH
What is "a threat?" EHHH
What is "an intruder?" EHH EHH EHH
What is a person, just like me, and just like you
Call the cops if you are in actual danger, not because folks is usin'
the wrong grill to barbeque
Because some Black people don't come back from that
Some Black people rightly get upset with the wrong kind of cop
And family and friends get left with the question of why did he
get shot?
Is my sister coming home? I just wanna see Daddy
And they wind up dead for what? Because they were just tryna
leave their Air BnB?
We belong
Our mere presence doesn't jeopardize your safety
So stop callin' the cops for your petty grievances cuz all you
callin' up is frustration and possible tragedy

It's Ok

Too many Black men wear their masculinity like a fresh pair of J's
Never wanting it to appear scuffed or worn
Will feel ashamed if it looks frayed
Will do anything to keep it together so it never gets torn

Too many Black men have poured cement into their tear ducts
Because God forbid some liquid starts to drain
Which is why brothas walking around with emotional reflux
Their hearts burn from backed up sadness and unreleased pain

But brotha, you da Bomb.com, you ain't got to be the grenade
Hard shell exterior with an internal fuse ready to detonate
Saying, "Nah, I'm kool," will give you no aid
And will just allow your four seasons of depression to marinate

Black man it is OK to cry
Unleash your tsunami of agony...ride the wave of release
You ain't gotta wear the mask of a tough guy
While your brothas and sistas are being gunned down by police

It's OK to get worked up over these supremely effed up scenarios
It's OK to take a second and live in that moment
Y tambien mis hermanos en los barrios
You ain't gotta dismiss your grief, you can own it

Your sistas are going through the same things too
But you should also find comfort in your brotherhood
Your shared experiences bring you together like glue
Dealing with the same racism, just in another hood

You can find strength in the very thing most people label as weak
A good cry can flush out the toxic emotions you are feeling
Confronting hidden pain can be just the help you seek
Letting it out can be step one of your healing

So I implore you to find some time for yourself
This whole "real men don't shed tears" is a lie
Suppressing your pain is detrimental to your health
So please, Black man, don't be afraid or ashamed to cry

Tree of Life

Black woman
You are the tree of life
Like a life-giving tree
Created to enhance and perpetually sustain the physical life of
humanity
The world constantly eats of your fruit
They take and take from you and you never fail to produce
Because your product is the result of you multiplied by the
strength of you, you are your own square root
Roots so deep they wrap around this universe
You set the standard for what a woman should be cuz you were
first
Tree of Life, with your thick branches and full leaves
So many try to copy and claim ownership of your assets, but no
one achieves
Black woman, you are the mother of eternity
You birthed this nation, this world, you are the definition of
maternity
This country wouldn't stand so tall if not for your sacrifices
And yet this country sits back while our Black mothers are in
crisis
Mama, Mama you know that I love you
I just want the rest of this country to love you too
Cuz see, everybody wants to be a Black woman
But nobody wants to be a Black woman
Nobody wants to live in the US and be three to four times more
likely to die from pregnancy-related complications
No one wants to birth Black babies who are more than twice as
likely as Whites to not make it to their 1-year birthday
celebrations
Mama, this is the status of Black motherhood and I just want
folks to know
Because this cannot continue, this cannot be our status quo
Black women are unbelievable!
With the ability to get bent out of shape, compressed in society,
and stretched to the limit
Yet bounce back stronger, a Black woman's blood got some spring
in it
She is fine
But she is human, so she is not like this all the time

Medical "professionals" are ignoring the stated pain of Black mothers and the results are tragic
Our pain is very real even though we have Black Girl Magic
We may be unbelievable, but it doesn't mean we should not be believed
As they did in the 1800's, some White folks are still out here thinking Black people don't feel pain and anxieties
Just because we make it look good don't mean we don't feel hurt
We've been conditioned to present as beautiful flowers without ever letting you see the turmoil embedded in our dirt
This mess of melanated maternal morbidity is not just a poor Black woman's problem, it stretches across the economic bracket
Medics not listening to Serena Williams almost caused her to never again pick up a tennis racket
Almost caused her to not be there to raise her little one
Black women in the wealthiest neighborhoods are more likely to die from maternity problems than White, Hispanic, and Asian moms in the poorest ones
Mama, Mama you know that I love you
I just want the rest of this country to love you too
Because no matter the income or class, you must consistently battle a certain kind of storm if Black woman is your name
And with so many storms, weathering of the body is to blame
Which is a premature deterioration of the bodies of Black women triggered by toxic stress
Living in an inescapable atmosphere of societal and systemic racism is causing Black women deadly distress
And this is not just Black women singing the blues
Fact: The effects of racism on the body are REAL, this is not fake news
Kalief Browder's mom died of a heart attack 16 months after missin' him
Eric Garner's daughter died from the results of the same when, like her dad, her brain had a lack of oxygen
The toxic stress of racism is eating Black women's bodies from within
But these are the homes we're supposed to grow our babies in
Mama!
Eclampsia is more severe in Black women and 60% more common, we are the majority
Stress from racism causes this and conditions like hypertension...is this how they keep us the minority?

You the tree of life, but just existing in this country is causing your premature deforestation
Every year 4000 of your Black seeds lose the chance to grow in this nation
America, wake up! This is a crisis! There's too much racial bias in the medical field
Invest in research on why Black moms and infants are dying at a disproportionally higher rate and then do something about the devastating results you yield
Believe Black women when they say they are in pain
We wouldn't be where we are in women's health if not for the experimental surgeries done on these women, without Novacaine
Black women you are life-giving trees
And if this country doesn't stop you and your seeds from dying, then nobody breathes
Love Black women, believe Black women, save Black women
Thank you

Passage

You came into my home and disrupted my space
Ironically, it was you that felt upset and attacked when you saw
my Black face
My afro, my heels, my military green shirt
To this day I don't know why my Blackness was the target that
triggered you to assert
Your White privilege while I was performing in a play on stage
What provoked the wolf inside you and released it from its cage
What made you want to huff and puff and blow our performance
to the ground
But we believe in doing work that's ground breaking so that
wasn't going down
You, a 30-40 year old White male sitting in the front row
With a t-shirt, muscles, tattoos, and support for Number 45?
Well, that part I don't know
I have no idea whether or not you voted for Donald Trump
But I can confirm that in the middle of our scene you loudly said,
"I don't mean to interrupt your Black Panther Party, and I'm not
Forrest Gump"
Under the influence of something, you talked about the world we
live in today
You even talked over us to ask questions about things you didn't
understand in the play
Like, "Who are they? I don't know who they are"
And then you went even further when you had already gone so far
Whatever impaired your judgement must have caused you to
think you were Rosa Parks' parakeet
Because you tried to mimic her words when you said "no" as the
house manager asked you to give up your front row seat
God has not given us a spirit of fear so who are you to dare give
one to me?
Never before had I been so scared of someone who was in such
close proximity
Is he going to jump on stage? Does he have a gun? These were all
questions that ran through my head
Trying to rapidly assess whether you were a threat or just White
and tasteless like a piece of Wonder Bread
You did all this yet somehow you were able to continue watching
the show

It wasn't until intermission when you were told you couldn't return and had to go

After a five minute racially motivated disturbance and a refusal to leave, you were allowed to freely walk out using your own two feet

Meanwhile, a few days before, two Black men were led out in handcuffs for not buying anything at Starbucks, literally four blocks down on the same street

Do you even realize the power of your fair skin? Or do you just benefit from it unawarely

They must call it fair skin because having it will most likely get you treated fairly

So we must have the unjust skin

Our melanin

Protects our cells from the many dangers of excess sun exposure

While simultaneously protecting the cells of private prisons by filling them with melanin so they never see closure

I was told you talked to a professor in the audience and apologized

You said the reason for your behavior was that the play made you feel attacked and marginalized

This pushed me over the edge and brought my anger and disbelief to level ten

YOU felt attacked and marginalized by this play when in real life innocent Black and Brown men

Are out here tryna survive in the Lion's den?!

Praying like Daniel that God will send an angel judge that will find them blameless in his sight

Meanwhile you acting out because of a playwright?

I guess it's scary to see the ugly aspects of your character in a play, stage fright

When it comes to dealing with racial issues, many White folks have an inability

R DiAngelo defines this as White Fragility

"A state in which even a minimum amount of racial stress becomes intolerable, triggering a range of defensive moves"

Like a White man who interrupts a play because he disapproves

But no need to fret, I have a cure for your fragility

It's free, you can grow it yourself, and it's called empathy

Which would allow you to actually *listen* to a different point of view

Instead of getting defensive and tackling every point like a
linebacker would do
You will never fully understand the racism that people of color
have to endure
But empathetic listening can allow you to try and understand it
more
Because the feelings associated with dealing with it are ones
you've felt before
As humans we all know anger, frustration, we all know pain
So to just completely dismiss someone's feelings because you
don't agree with how they got them is simply inhumane
This play forced you to confront and challenge your views
But if you continue to fight perspective with animus, you will
always lose
You made me live a nightmare in the place I actualize my dreams,
the stage
But I'm grateful you did because I found a lesson in your outrage
I learned Whiteness can be as fragile as a baby's bones, but strong
enough to pull you out of trouble
And that you'll go blind if you only look at things inside your own
bubble
The play was called "Passage," so let me pass this on to you
If you open your mind and close your mouth, you just might
understand what it's like to wear a different shoe

Body Positive

I look in my mirror and I see
That my breasts are spilling out of my bra
They smush out of the bottom like melty marshmallows after you
trap them between two graham crackers and a piece of chocolate
This piece of chocolate has had too much caramel
Too many peanuts
Has answered the question, "Hungry?" with "Why wait?" so
many times that her mirror now Snickers at the reflection it
presents
My mirror has fun laughing at me in my own house
A fun house mirror distorting my love of the ever fluctuating body
it reflects
My breasts did not do this six months ago
Did not take up more space than they were allotted
Now if only Black women were allowed to be an itty bitty like my
bigger titty, but that's an aside
A size, times two or three, is how much my body has expanded in
the past six months
Like a sponge swollen with water
Except the water is fat
And I wish I could just wring my body out
Watch the pounds drip drip out my pores like Cardi B
Shoulda did more cardio
Yo, shoulda been at the gym like, "Sweat on my neck stay
drippin', I need ice"
But I didn't
Now my knockers are tapping on my chest like
"Knock, knock"
And I'm like, "Who's there?"
And they're like, "A bigger size"
And I'm like, "A bigger size? Who?"
"You!"
"Bish, where?"
"YOU are a bigger size!"
But I don't want to believe them
So every day I bury my treasures in a chest that's too small
hoping no one would notice my excess bounty
That no one would notice the transformation of people's
Instagram comments to me over the past 24 weeks
"Yaas, body! Lookin' fit and fab!"

Has been replaced with
"Loving your color coordination!"
Social media celebrates you when you reach your #BodyGoals
But can also immortalize the backslide
Folks can flick through your pics like a flip book
And watch your image expand through your time line
There is no protection for folks' exposure to your SCF
Subtle Chronological Failure
When they can just tap into you at various stages of your life
At various stages of your weight loss journey
And I be feeling lost on this journey
Tryna reach the finish line of fitness but it seems I'm just stuck on a track
Running steady, to running slowly, to not running at all
And next thing you know, I'm back
To where I started, sometimes even further behind
With a bigger behind
But that part can stay
I just want to get these pounds off, for me
And for on camera roles that don't prefer rolls
But ain't you posed to be a role model?
And Black?
And strong?
With poetry that models body positivity?
Negative
Black women ain't got to be strong all the damn time, cuz nobody is
And honestly, if I can't be honest in my own poetry, then where can I be?
Where else can I be weak while seeking strength in the vulnerability that comes from speaking spoken words of my insecurity?
Speakin' bout how six months ago a racial trauma kicked me out my comfort zone
Had me seeking solace in comfort foods
But how that turned my wardrobe into a misfit in my closet cuz my clothes started fittin' uncomfortable
They say, "You should be ashamed...there are girls actually struggling, dreaming they were your size"
But you wouldn't deny an upgrade to your vehicle just because the person at the bus stop wishes they had your ride
My personal struggle is real for me

In my opinion, part of body shaming is shaming me for not being happy with where I am with my body
I love me, but I can't act like I don't have fitness and health goals I'm tryna move toward
Also, as an actress my body is a part of my resume so I'm just tryna put my best foot forward
If this was too forward then I do not apologize
Cuz just saying these thoughts out loud has done more for my body positivity than you can realize

GenTro of the Dance Flo'

The dance floor is my home away from home
I like it to be spacious so I have the freedom to roam
Not crowded with chicks surrounding me like I'm in a coup
I need space to Al B and cook up my Chicken Noodle Soup
Wit' a soda on the side
Like in my house, I feel best when I got my husband by my side
He's not my partner in crime, but my partner in life and dance
It's like there's no one else in the world when we get in our
dancing trance
Whether we doin' a sexy salsa or some Cotton Eye Joe, it don't
matter the circumstance
We visit our home away from home whenever we get the chance
I get my whole life when I'm on the dance flo'
Which is why it kills me when people interrupt my dance flow
These people go to the bar and buy, buy, buy until they've had too
much to drink
They're usually White with dance moves that are not in sync
They spot the home we've made from across the room, then get
closer for a real tour
They move into our space and thus begins the gentrification of
the dance floor
I first experienced this type of GenTro when I was a college
freshman
My body answering the call of the music when a White girl began
to question
"How do you do that? When I try it I look like such a fool"
I'd read about it, but it was my first time, in real life, seeing a
White girl tryna steal my cool
It was live action appropriation
Had she just stopped by to say "I love your dance moves" it would
have been welcomed appreciation
But no, she showed up unannounced and stepped into my home
Tried to take the moves from my body and make them her own
Unfortunately, this is what some White women will often do
Use their Massacard to swipe things from our bodies, then decline
to give credit when it's due
So while I love to give, the dance floor is not where I do charity
Book a studio, pay me, then I'll answer all your dance questions
'til you have clarity
Cuz when I'm in my second home I just wanna be me

Whether I'm with my husband, or a group of friends, I just wanna be free
Melodies melt melancholy moods
Funk fixes frequent feuds
So when you bull doze your way into my dance circle
Like the bulldozers in DC did to Logan Circle
While you flail your arms and shout "Woo" in my face
Invading my little area when you already take up so much space
I can't help but feel frustration
You tryna Harlem Shake, but I'm thinking about its gentrification
Black and brown communities slowly being replaced by folks that look like you, and you, and you too, that's a hard pill to swallow
Even on Harlem's most famous dance floor, we got U2 playing the Apollo
So if you pull out your phone when I'm dancing with my husband, Imma be like, "Really tho'?"
No, you can't use our joy for likes on your Instagram video
Our culture is live but you can't use it to transform your profile from basic milk to Yoplait
If I say, DJ, yo play "Throw Dem Bows" I bet chu then you'll want to stay away
Cuz while fighting GenTro in reality is hard, on the dance floor Imma stand my ground
Imma hit chu wit' these dance moves while I drop it to the ground
And let's be clear, I'm no dancing professional
I just find allowing my body to get lost in the music to be super enjoyable
It's cardio, it's a good time, it's therapy
I be in my own magical world, so please just beware of me
We can share a few glances, wave our hands in the air
We could even do a dance or two if I'm over here and you're over there
Just please do not break into my dance aura
Give me some space, you are not Steve, I am not Laura
Whether I'm doing the Shiggy, the Wop, or the heel-toe
Do not just put me in your video
Do not enter my dance home, cuz that's a no-no
Please, just don't gentrify the dance flo'

Popped Culture

I saw an article on the interwebs, "The 90 Best Shows of the 90's" was the header
I read that list and said, "The writer must not have known no better"
Must not have known the people who grew up in my hood
Cuz if he did, then there's no way that he could
Leave out so many of our favorite shows
But when it comes to deciding what's an American favorite, this is how it often goes
White culture is the standard, the default, the mainstream
So while our stuff may be the hottest, it's invisible to White America, it is just steam
"Justine, Justine!"
Never seen an episode of Frasier, but best believe I can quote lines and do dances from the Cosby Show
Do you know about Justine becoming Myra and wanting to be an Urkel instead of a Huxtable?
RIP
How dare you make a list of the best shows from my childhood and not include Tamera Campbell and Tia Landry?
Growing up with no Sister Sisters, or brothers, Tia and Tamera were like family to me
They were the heroes I wrote about in grade school, they were who I wanted to be
That show played such an important part of my life, yet it didn't even make the list
And it surely wasn't the only show placed on the blacklist
For us to be highly ranked and recognized we gotta have a separate Black List
Yet some of their shows wouldn't even exist without ours, get into that plot twist
1993, when my community wanted to relate to a show about us, living in the city, Living Single said, "I'll be there for you"
But in 1994, the creator of Friends said, "I'll be there for you too"
They say imitation is the sincerest form of flattery
But when White folk do it to Black folk it just reminds us of their history of banditry
They ain't make the cut, but me and my friends always had on Moesha, Jamie Foxx, The BLACK Parent 'Hood, and a Different World when we was in the house

Before NCIS, LL Cool J was always on In the House
But honestly, it ain't this little list that upsets me, it's what it represents
Because when you can't quote most of the shows on this list, some White folk think you have no common sense
It's common for me to be in mostly White spaces and feel left out the loop
Them laughing at jokes I don't get reminds me that I'm not really part of their group
The way they whip their heads around to stare at me like the Exorcist
Eyes bulging out, hands over their hearts, absolutely incredulous
"You never watched The Simpsons?! But they're America's favorite family!"
Well, America hired my relatives to be the help, so I'm not surprised I was never introduced to this branch of the fam tree
I was born here, so I do come from a proud, American family
But the only Simpson I knew was OJ, I was watching Proud Family
Proud Family, Proud Fam-a-lee
They push my buttons when they assume I know parts of their culture when they barely know a quarter of mine
Me not knowing Mr. Burns is a cardinal sin
But you not knowing LaCienega is just fine
Funny how on this list The Simpsons found themselves in the spot of number one
But if I were to make the list and you were looking for a spot for these yellow characters, you would find none
The culture you chew on may pop in your bubble, but that doesn't mean it's popular to me
Jokes about your pop culture will often leave me staring blankly
So frankly, all I'm tryna say is don't assume I know your pop references because the people in your circle do
And honestly, I have no problem with my culture being outside the "American" box, that's actually where I'm most comfortable

Wakanda Forever

When the cast list for Black Panther came out, complete with
headshots, I thought it was fan fiction
I literally did not believe a Marvel superhero movie was gonna
show such a Black depiction
In every actor's picture I saw myself reflected again and again
and again
Here were these talented Black actors, all with gorgeous dark skin
And then the trailer came out and I almost lost my mind
They lived in an advanced, self-sufficient African country,
untouched by White people, and everyone's hair was the same
texture as mine
I saw shaved heads, braids, afros, bantu knots, Black hairstyles
galore
I appreciated seeing crowns I've rocked on my head before
Then the actors showed up for the official screening, showed up
and showed out
Letting the world know what Black Excellence is all about
They worked the purple carpet in colors that made their melanin
pop, as if in a frying pan
It was so Black, I'm surprised there were no burning crosses
outside from the Ku Klux Klan
It was the memo that no Black person could say they didn't get
It was the letter sent home from school saying that when we go
on our Wakanda field trip
You must wear your Blackest outfit
You could go all Panther Party, with leather and berets, as a
tribute to folks like Huey P
Or you could come ankara'd down, smelling like incense and oils,
looking like African royalty
I chose the latter and on Friday, February 16, 2018, I went to
Wakanda with my king
No movie theatre experience has ever made me feel such a thing
To see so much representation
Made me feel like I was getting a small piece of reparation
They owed us this movie
For the Black kids labeled superpredators that never got to see
superheroes with their same color skin
For the Black girls wanting a princess whose happiness wasn't
dependent on a prince stepping in
We needed this movie

Every time we went, we didn't just go to the theatre, we went to Wakanda
With turbocharged joy and on one Accord like a Honda
We watched that thing 'til there was not a credit or extra scene left, like when you wipe the bowl clean after mixing cake batter
Trying to savor every second of living in a fictional reality where Black Lives Always Matter
Sure, there was conflict and death, as present in any society
But in Wakanda, just having Black skin was not cause for anxiety
It was cause for celebration
Stark was the contrast when I left T'Challa and went back to having Trump as the leader of my nation
Stark was the contrast between the image of Black women in Wakanda and the ones I've seen in films of the past
When I saw the king's armed forces, the Dora Milaje, my soul began to croon like Etta James, "At Last"
This was no bald head scallywag, ain't got no hair in back
These were no whores, or slaves, or women battling the effects of crack
These were bold, bald, Black, badasses battling and protecting the most advanced nation on the globe
I had to think, am I really seeing this or is there an impairment in my occipital lobe?
With those spears they poked holes in the myth that short hair and dark skin equals ugly and masculine
Eviscerating foes while being fierce and feminine
This was more than a movie, it was a loud statement to Hollywood
That yes, we can do all the things you thought we never could
Like be the 3rd highest-grossing domestic movie of all time
Like make more than 1.2 billion in 26 days, shifting all types of paradigms
For five straight weeks Black Panther was at number one
It was the highest-grossing film by a Black director ever done
This and more accomplished with a cast that was all Blackity-dark-chocolate-Black
So, Hollywood, stop sleeping on positive, Black narratives becoming blockbusters, become an insomniac
Cuz we are hungry for more stories and casts like these...and clearly the rest of the world is too
Stop trying to force feed us these white bread stories that are stale and difficult to chew

Out of Black Panther came representation and opportunity, which people of color need more of in this society
And not just in Hollywood, but in positions that change policies and systems and break vicious cycles like those of poverty
I applaud every fearless person who was a part of this Black Panther endeavor
It is an experience I will never forget and will keep close to my heart
Wakanda Forever

Over and Over Again

I've been in love with a Black man since before a Black man was
president
Since 2005 you have graffiti'd your name on the walls of my heart
over and over again
Our love story is both old and new
Hieroglyphics translated by Alexa
It's futuristic cuz I can't see mine without you in it
And it is a story I am honored to keep creating with you
You, my Black man
My Daddy is a Black man
And his Daddy was a Black man
And the very first man was a Black man
Created in the image of Thee Man Upstairs
So loving you is historic
And Biblical
And familiar
And destined
Black man, I love you from the top of your head
To the soles of my feet
Your head is amazing
Your brain is exquisite
I'm a library of your wisdom
You fill me with pages of your beautiful nuanced thought over and
over again
Even when I don't wanna hear it
Even when it calls me out on my BS
Cuz I know every time we talk I'm speaking your love language
So whenever we converse, I know that's just you lovin' on me
Even when I don't agree
Whenever you speak your Black Thoughts to me I feel The Roots
of our love grow deeper in my body
And loving you is deep
Cuz loving a Black man, in this country, is not easy
Knowing that when I look at you I see husband, but they see
guilty
I hear intellect, they hear thug
I feel love, they feel threatened
A White man's life insurance is found in his skin
An assurance in the power of his skin color that is not found in
melanin

But God has not given us a spirit of fear
So we replace "goodbyes" with "I love yous" and pray for your safety over and over again
Every microaggression you're forced to swallow on a daily because of your skin gets pushed down to your hips
But when you get home I'm happy to be your release
Ain't nothin' micro about the aggression you put into me
Cuz I like it a little rough
Tough love is sometimes the best love when you make love consensually
And sensuously
Activating all 5 of my senses simultaneously
You arch my blackbone when we
Bone of my bone
Flesh of my flesh
We are one and become one over and over again
Black man you are my back bone
Being in love with you is like finding length in my spine
You build me up
You tuck words of encouragement in my vertebrae so I stand tall in any situation
You believe in my dreams more than a kid believes in Santa
And baby, you are a true gift
You see what I'm building and support me like a beam
I will always select you, Black man, to be on my team
To be in my corner
Sharing laughs like folks share beers over happy hour
I choose you, Black man, over and over again
Because you choose me, over and over again
You've gone from my prom date to my life mate
And still
I choose you, Black man
I choose you
Over
and
over
again

My Voice, My Choice

Hiiiiii! My name is Jaylene Clark Owens and this is not my voice
This is not my normal register
This is a choice
This cadence creeps unconsciously into my vocal box cavity
And uuuuuuuummmmmmm
All of a sudden my voice begins to lift
Wraps up my vocal chords and presents them to you like a gift
Making my voice higher and sweeter, thus more pleasing to your ear palette
Instead of rough, harsh sounds that play on your ear drums with a mallet
Yeah, this is not how I would normally sound
Wow, I didn't even realize I was actually trying to hold the real me down
To suppress me, so you can trust me
I wonder if my voice is so high you can't hear the irony
I do it automatically
I just pop this voice in without thinking
The same way you would pop on a life vest if you were sinking
It saves me
From being too Harlem, too deep, too Black

snap

But girl, you is alla that
This voice is too fly to be left sittin in the cut like a cul-de-sac
Waiting
For a friend, a family member, your cousin
Why can't the voice you use with an employer be the same one you use with your husband?

* snap*

Becaaaause, as a woman, we're conditioned from birth to be meek
Taught that the man should have the most strength so we even make our voices weak
Becaaaause, as a Black person, we're taught from birth to be non-threatening

So we quiet the bass of the African drum that strums our vocal chords 'til silence is deafening
Becaaaause, as a female who is Black we are labeled Angry Black Woman, and even when we're not, we get the name even still
So we Kenny G our Louis Armstrongs until we sound tranquil

snap

Like a tranquilizer gun, temporarily sedating yourself so you may be easily handled, true self on mute
But this voice matters too, hands up, don't shoot
This voice, has roots, in New York City
It's gritty
Knows that life is not always pretty
But it is ever beautiful in its boldness, never drowning in self-pity
This voice is indicative of where you are from, but that should have no relevance
Because your home of Harlem should not be indicative of your level of intelligence
Habitually, we are told our Blackness cannot enter White spaces without a code
Without

* snap*

code-switching

snap

Without it, their minds would be glitching
Trying to compute our vernacular
But this voice is spectacular
It is the purest form of your articulated thoughts, like rainwater after impurities have been vaporized
That other voice is not the real thing, just poorly plagiarized you
Universalized you
Stop treating your voice like the cat that disappears when company's around, boo

But I know you feel most vocally comfortable when you around ya best friends
Finger waves becomes commas and claps encapsulate words like bookends

snap

But you can't just roll your neck and refuse to articulate in a professional setting

snap

mouth click

Why not? But it's okay to upspeak so that everything sounds like a question, I'm betting

snap

Why? Because it makes you sound ghetto, uneducated, I don't think that's a big mystery

snap

Ghetto? That is a left over ancestral sound from the clicking languages found in the southern African tribes, that *mouth click* is my history

snap

Well, you can't always show all your cards...sometimes you need your poker face

snap

But this face is Black 24/7...I can't turn it on and off based on time and place
This voice is yours so own it
Stand up for its validity in powerful places, be its proponent

snap

Maybe I won't go full Harlem bird, but I'll let my voice fly
Breaking this ingrained habit will be difficult but I'll give it a try
So hiiiiii *clears throat* **hi, my name is Jaylene Clark Owens**
and this is *my voice *clears throat** **voice**
Love it or hate it, that is your choice

ABOUT THE POET

Jaylene Clark Owens is a highly acclaimed poet, as well as an AUDELCO and Barrymore Award winning actress, from Harlem, NY. She is a first place Apollo Theater Amateur Night winner for her poetry. Jaylene is proudly one of the co-writers of *Renaissance in the Belly of a Killer Whale*, the award winning, spoken word infused play about gentrification in Harlem.

Made in the USA
Columbia, SC
05 January 2025

51287672R00045